About the Author

Drake Hubert is an American-born author of both fiction and non-fiction. He enjoys writing fantastical stories and essays that explore the darkest areas of life, especially those which relate to love, relationships, and interpersonal demons. The young author wishes to help readers gain an appreciation for how important our connections to other people in this world are.

A Painted Lie

Drake Aidan Hubert

A Painted Lie

Olympia Publishers
London

www.olympiapublishers.com
OLYMPIA PAPERBACK EDITION

A CIP catalogue record for this title is
available from the British Library.

ISBN: 978-1-80439-175-4

This is a work of fiction.
Names, characters, places and incidents originate from the writer's
imagination. Any resemblance to actual persons, living or dead, is
purely coincidental.

First Published in 2023

Olympia Publishers
Tallis House
2 Tallis Street
London
EC4Y 0AB

Printed in Great Britain

FOREWORD

I feel that this story needs a foreword, but I am not quite sure how to write it.

There are some points I want to make and people I want to thank. However, there is no particularly eloquent way of doing so that I have in my mind. As such, allow me to release a volley of ideas.

Ever since I wrote my first novel, I have struggled to come up with a story that would comprise the same amount of words as it (over fifty-five thousand). All other stories that I have wanted to tell would not take nearly that many words. Eventually, I convinced myself to commit to one of these stories regardless and see where it takes me. And where it took me was a place where I had a short story of which I was very proud. A story that I took certainly more pride in than my novel. When I started writing it, I knew publishers wouldn't take so kindly to such a short story, and I know that now, with the finished story in front of me. And that's…okay. The amount of words used to tell this story were the amount of words necessary, not the amount of words to hit some mystical threshold that says: "Now you can take pride in this work. Now you can show it to the world and show them how great you are." This is a short story, and it's a better story because of it.

There is a virtually endless number of people that I *could* thank right now. In the broadest possible sense, I extend a thank you to every person that is in my life or has been in my life, for each one of you has played a part in making me who I am. By making me who I am, you've made me capable of telling this story, for *I* wouldn't exist, if not for *you*. But the people in my life don't want to hear that! They want to hear their name be called out directly. I can't possibly name every person, but there are some that I must point out individually.

To begin, I must thank my immediate family, the trio of people who make my life worth living for every day. My dad, Matt Hubert, is also a writer and my biggest inspiration. My mom, Julie Duke, is my number one supporter. And my sister, Valeska Hubert, is the biggest source of positivity and warmth in my life - she makes me want to keep moving.

I want to express my appreciation for those who have been the biggest supporters of my work up to this point. Thank you, Emily Swanson, whose praise and support has left me in tears. Thank you, Halle Chambers, for convincing me that my stories had value when I was most wary. Thank you, Luke Isom, for your perpetual and warm support for all of my writing aspirations. And a thank you to Jordan Guzman, who created an environment and circumstances that allowed my writing to flourish, all the while being invested in and supportive of my work.

Again, thank you to all of my friends, acquaintances, and enemies who I didn't name. You all are, in a literal sense, the world to me. Without any further pretext, allow me to tell you a story.

1

I've spent a great many evenings sitting next to the front window of the living room, fastened to my personal table and chair which I use to create my paintings. There was little to see out the window, and virtually nothing was ever different. However, a set of woods lie about a hundred yards away, just beyond the now empty field of crops of our farm, and they alone always gave me inspiration for new painting ideas. I suppose seeing the woods made me start to think about what's inside of them: birds, insects, deer, rivers, and flowers. So much beauty, all entailed just beyond the trees.

This evening was no different, I sat at my table next to the window and worked on a painting of a bird nest with newborn hatchlings high in a tree. The sun was beginning to make its descent as Pa remained outside, using what little natural light he had left in the day to finish up farm work. Pa didn't like that I painted, and I didn't like working on the farm. However, he had decided that he would buy the supplies I needed and allow me to paint *if* I helped out; otherwise, I wouldn't be able to. That is a deal that I have bashfully accepted for the majority of my life.

Even with his nominal consent to my painting, he would still seize any opportunity he could to ridicule my paintings and criticize me for putting time into them in the first place. That's why this time in the evening was my favorite time to do it. The house was empty and quiet, and he was outside, not around to give me a hard time for doing it. As the sky became plagued with the blackness of the night, I braced myself for Pa's inevitable entrance through the front door. And right on schedule, the door swung open, and Pa walked in.

His boots made a thud as they hit the rug just in front of the door. He reached his burly hands down to take them off before going any further. The bottoms of them were caked with dirt. Behind his thick grey and black beard was a stern look, complimented by squinty brown eyes. His attire was always basically the same: a plaid flannel shirt and jeans, only varying in the color of the flannel. His only accessory was a crude necklace that was adorned with a small key. His silence exclaimed his exhaustion as he stood at the door.

"I'm grabbing a shower, then I'll make dinner. I'll want you at the kitchen table by then," he said without looking at me. I squeamishly stared up at him from the paper, anxiously waiting for him to walk away. He reached down, grabbed his boots, and carried them with him upstairs. A quiet sigh of relief emitted from me as I went back to the paper to continue my piece. I had experienced these circumstances so much in the past that I had learned exactly how long Pa would take to get back downstairs, and how long I would have to continue painting.

On a night like tonight, a terribly frustrating dilemma happened to me during this period of time. The painting was nearing completion. If I rushed, I could certainly finish it. But if I was appreciative of my time, I would not. My brain ultimately deemed it easier to not think about the dilemma and to not work on the painting at all, as my head was pulled to look out the window into the dark night. The porch light just outside the front door helped illuminate about thirty feet out from the window, but there was little interest to be seen in that range. Beyond the light was what mattered: The forest. It remained discernible in the night as the sky sat a mere hint brighter than the pitch-black trees. As I stared out at the trees, a mixture of thoughts about what to do with the painting along with fantastical daydreaming going through my mind, and two faint orbs of light spawned between the two trees. The orbs appeared about seven feet off the ground and took on the shape of eyes.

The eyes were not squinted, nor angled; they weren't malicious. The eyes were not a horrific red color like that out of a horror film, nor were they a mysterious, simple white. They were a calming, almost innocent, light blue. I was entirely too far away from them to make out any of their details, but all I knew was that I did not feel threatened by them. I felt entranced by them.

"About ready?" a gravelly voice behind me said, breaking my trance.

I frantically turned around to see Pa looking over at me from the kitchen.

"It's almost finished. Get ready," he said. I looked down at my painting. I had gotten no further than where I was when Pa first walked in. I glanced outside to the trees, in search of the eyes, but they were gone. Quickly, I placed my soiled paint brushes into a cup of water to soak before heading over to the kitchen sink to wash my hands. As Pa started to put food onto a plate, I assumed my position at the chair of the kitchen table facing the window. This chair was the one I always sat in, and Pa always sat in the one across from it. The third chair, which faced the living room, was to remain empty, always.

I sat in silence as my leg bounced up and down quietly, beneath the table, bringing to light my anxiety that I wanted so desperately to keep secret. Pa turned toward the table, carrying a plate in each hand. He placed one down in front of me, allowing me to bear witness to the less than pleasant sight that was tonight's dinner. Half of the plate contained lackluster scrambled eggs, devoid of any seasoning, while the other half of the plate contained thick-cut, room temperature bologna. I couldn't decide what was worse: eggs as part of dinner, or the fact that it was eggs with bologna of all things. Pa sat the other plate down in front of his chair before turning back toward the counter and grabbing two glasses of water that he had already poured. Just like the plates, he placed one glass in front of me and one at his chair before taking his seat.

"Sorry it's not milk, we ran out. I'll have us fill the bottles up in the morning," Pa remarked before taking his first bite. I had to conceal my sense of shock as I swallowed a sip of water. That was the kindest way he had talked to me all day, if not all week. I spent a brief moment deliberating whether to respond or not.

"Oh," I started before letting out a small, rather forced chuckle. "That's okay. It's not the end of the world." We both went silent for a spell as we ate some of our food.

"The tractor is still out in the field. You'll have to

drive it out of there while I tend to the chickens. After that, there's some wood out back that needs—"

"Can we not talk about it right now?" I found myself cutting him off, much to both of our surprise. "You spend all day out there working. Why not think and talk about something else? We'll figure out what needs to be done in the morning." Pa let out a small sigh at the comment.

"The farm is my life, boy. Day or night, rain or shine, whether I'm out there or sitting in here at the table, it's what I think about." He spoke without looking at me, and nor did I look at him. We both kept our heads down toward our plates.

"How do you think I feel about painting?" I remarked, prompting Pa to raise his eyes toward me. Feeling his gaze, I nervously looked up at him as well.

"Yeah... but the farm isn't a waste of time," he proclaimed, letting his gaze linger on me for a moment as I was compelled to look him in the eyes. Our mock staring contest subsided a few moments later as we went back to eating. Not another word was spoken for the rest of dinner.

There was, always, a wonderful wave of relief that washed over me after Pa finished eating and dismissed himself from the table. He went upstairs to drift off to sleep while I stayed downstairs. It was my job to wash the dishes. When I went to clean Pa's plate, I was taken aback by how little he had eaten. He was sometimes so exhausted at night he hardly had the energy to eat. As I scrubbed away at the dishes, I heard the sounds of muffled voices upstairs, coming from Pa's TV. His room harbored the only TV in the house, but he never actually watched it. The only reason he had it was because the noise from it helped him to fall asleep. I was never quite sure whether the sound of the TV turning on meant I needed to be quiet because he was going to sleep, or if I could be noisy because the TV would drown out everything else. Either way, the noisiest thing I ever did was accidentally make the floorboards creak under my feet as I walked.

Once I finished up with the dishes, I made my way upstairs myself. At the top of the stairs were three doors. The door straight ahead was to the bathroom, the door to the right was Pa's room, and the door to the left was my room. I stepped inside my room and flipped on the light switch. Every time I stopped to take in my room, I felt a great deal of sadness and disappointment. There was virtually no personalization to be found. I had a bed composed of grey sheets, blankets, and a pillowcase. I had a wooden dresser and desk, both of which had many scratches and weathered spots indicative of their ancestry. I had sometimes considered painting at the desk in my room, but my bed sat next to the window, and I didn't want to paint in a spot where I couldn't see outside properly. I flipped off my light and crawled into bed, looking up at the ceiling. There, taped to the off-white painted surface, was the one piece of personalization my room had, gently visible in the moonlight.

A painting, certainly the painting I was most proud of, and perhaps the only one I was proud of at all. It depicts a bird's nest, situated finely along a tree branch. The nest houses baby birds, but not for long. The three birds inside the nest are all pitched along its edge, spreading their wings out as they prepare to fly away and live their own life.

Though I felt a sense of pride from the painting, it was not hung up as a way of showing off skills. I think the real reason I taped it to the ceiling was that it inspired me. On the days I felt ashamed of my painting skills, or, in particularly awful cases, the days where I didn't paint at all, looking up and seeing that piece never failed to make me feel better. Once I received my adequate dose of joy and encouragement for the night, I turned my head toward my window and began to gently doze off.

For most of my life, my dreams were never simply good or bad. They never were just okay either. It was always a barrage of visions, where some made me feel good, others euphoric, some bad, others heartbreaking. In a way, it made me rather admire sleep. I was always excited to sleep because I never knew what emotions I would feel, or for how long, but I knew no emotion would last forever, and that was relieving.

This wonderful sleep pattern, however, found itself dissipating in recent days. It felt like, with each passing night, my dreams became more and more negative and were evolving into something terrifying. It was beginning to reach the point that I was afraid, on some level, to sleep. Tonight was no different. As my eyes closed and my head lay against the pillow, the now routine war between my body and mind began; my body yearned for sleep, and my mind desperately begged me to stay awake. As fate had it, my body always emerged the victor, just as it did tonight.

Though I cannot recall what I was dreaming about on this night, it must not have been good, for I awoke in a panicked state, sweating profusely, in the middle of the night. I desperately reached over to my bedside table to grab the glass of water I always kept on it at night. I began to relentlessly take down large gulps, trying to cool off and calm down. As I chugged away at the water, I suddenly heard something that sent an otherworldly feeling through my entire body. From outside the window, I heard my name being called.

"Jay…" a deep, ethereal voice emitted. It was as though the voice had come from the sky itself as it echoed in my ears. I was surprised to have recognized the name, for I hadn't been referred to by it in years. I frantically pressed my face up against my window, looking outside to see where the noise came from. I saw nothing, neither on the ground nor in the sky. My brain started to provide me with the wonderfully relieving thought that the voice was merely my imagination as a result of still being half asleep.

But just as I began to believe that line of thought, my eyes caught something emerging from the trees of the forest.

A towering figure who harbored, no less than seven feet off the ground, the calming blue eyes which I had sworn to have seen earlier in the night. Its steps against the ground were powerful. From where I stood, there was a light tapping sound, but to hear them at all from this distance was testimony to the creature's incredible size. The creature's steps were not from human-like feet, but from hooves, like that of a bull. As it moved further out of the woods, and closer to the house, more of its features became visible.

The creature's legs and torso were covered with fur, and incredibly muscular. Wrapped around its waist and draped in front of its legs, there was a long piece of cloth-like material. It was not a material that could be replicated; it was composed of a barrage of colors and had an ominous glow to it. It was as though the universe itself was encapsulated inside the cloth. At its torso, there were two similar pieces of cloth, each draped around one of its shoulders, crossing over one another to create an x shape in front of its chest. These pieces, just like the piece at its legs, resembled something galactic with their colorful appearance and glow.

The creature's arms were equally fur-covered and muscle-bound. Its hands were large, with lanky fingers. Each finger was adorned with a claw that carried the same colorful appearance as its clothes. Much more important and staggering: its right hand gripped a large handle, the handle of a weapon, the blade of which was concealed in the darkness behind its shoulder.

Finally, the creature took the last necessary steps to fully illuminate and reveal itself in the moonlight. Its head blended seamlessly with the rest of its body, for it had the fur-covered head of a bull. A large ring hung from its nose, a ring that matched its clothing and claws. Likewise, its two horns, which pointed straight up to the sky, were composed of the galactic appearance at their tips, but were bone at their base. The weapon which sat on its shoulder was a massive ax, the blade wider than its head. The entire blade was a pristine, silver metal, except for its edges which held the colorful glow of its clothes, horns, and claws. Once the creature was fully illuminated, it stopped and stared up at me before speaking again.

"Jay…" it repeated itself as its eyes began to glow.

The glow was utterly entrancing. It felt as though I lost control of my body as I put on my jeans and a shirt, not bothering with shoes, before making my way downstairs and out the front door. I was not at all noise conscious or afraid of waking Pa during all the motion, my sole motivation was to get outside as quickly as possible. Once I was out the front door, I felt in control of myself again, but I continued moving toward the creature, only now it felt like a deliberate decision.

I could not hope to possibly explain to myself why I felt drawn toward such, by all reasonable accounts, an intimidating figure. Even as I walked toward the creature, thoughts went through my head accusing me of sleepwalking, dreaming, or downright insanity. Was I really outside, or was I only outside in my head? The creature remained stationary. It lingered calmly, watching me with its cool, blue eyes as I made my way toward it. As I started to become aware of just how far the creature was still, I felt my legs beginning to move faster and faster. Having no caution for my bare feet, I spent no time or energy looking down at where I was going. My eyes were locked with the creature's; I am not certain that I could even blink.

My failure to heed caution along my path came to haunt me, as I felt my heel glide over the blade of a small garden scythe that lay in the chopped down field. My body, however, found itself completely unyielding to the pain. I continued along my path toward the creature, leaving a narrow trail of blood behind me. I found myself continuing to put weight on the injured foot; it hurt each time I did, but if not for the trail of blood there would be no signs of injury from my behavior. After what felt simultaneously like seconds and centuries, I came within about ten feet of the creature and stopped.

My head began to tilt itself up in order to see the creature's bull-like head which towered above me. The creature finally put in some effort of its own, beginning to step forward to close the remaining gap between itself and me. As it moved, I began to come to my senses in a marginal way, as I realized what kind of creature I was looking at: a minotaur.

The sudden knowledge that what I was looking at was something straight out of a myth caused me to be both humored and anxious about my situation.

"This can't be real," I found myself uttering as the creature came to a stop, leaving no more than a foot of space between itself and me. I begin to frantically pace back and forth, leaving splotches of blood on the ground where I stepped. "You're, you're a…" I started as I continued pacing, glancing up at the creature and back at the ground repeatedly. "You're a minotaur!" I blurted out, stopping for a moment to look the beast in the eyes. It's way of responding was a mere huff, sending a visible gust of air out its snout.

"So, this is a dream, right?" I asked myself, looking up at the creature as though it would come out and tell me if it was. "This is just one super detailed dream, and I'm gonna wake up back in bed." A smile came across my face as I managed to assure myself that I had figured out what was going on and that all this would be over once I woke up. But such reassurance faded as quickly as it came, for I suddenly recalled seeing the beast's eyes in the trees before going to bed.

"But I saw you when I was awake," I started, bringing myself to a stop as though to lecture the creature. "So those eyes..." A sudden explanation occurred to me that restored my assurance in myself that this was all in mind. "Those eyes were just my imagination, and now my dreaming brain is imagining those eyes belong to you, a thing I'd only read about in a fantasy book!" My eyes widened and I pointed at the creature with confidence as I felt that I had figured out what it was. The creature began to take steps toward me, leaving virtually no space between itself and me. My face quickly lost its confidence, and my hand went down to my side as I anxiously looked up at the creature. Though I was convinced this was a dream, I still felt afraid. The creature blinked its eyes for what seemed like the first time, before speaking.

"Do you hear the sound of my steps and feel the strength of my presence?" it asked with its bellowing voice which ever more seemed to come from the sky itself. I found myself briefly perplexed by the question, but my confusion was cut short by the terrifying sight of the creature lifting up its ax. Before I could even turn around to run, the creature sent the ax down toward my head.

2

I awoke from my slumber in a chaotic frenzy. As I frantically waved my arms around in front of me and my legs flopped around as though they were attempting to run, I toppled out of my bed onto the cold, hardwood floor. I grunted with pain as the sensation of my head, now throbbing, brought me back to my senses. My eyes closed and I released a heavy sigh as I realized that I was, in fact, not dead, nor did I have a massive ax wound in my head. With a noteworthy struggle, I lifted myself off of the ground and onto my feet. Haphazardly, my hands began to reorganize my bed and blankets as my eyes stared out the window toward the woods. I mildly laughed at myself for believing that any of what I had just dreamed was real. Once my bed was made, I began to walk toward my bedroom door, but I came to a halt as I felt a strange sensation on the bottom of my foot.

It was not a feeling of pain, nor even discomfort. It was virtually indescribable. I placed my hand against a wall to support myself as I lifted my foot up to examine it.

Along my heel, there was a massive scar in a slightly curved shape. It resembled the injury that the scythe in the dream caused me, had that injury been given weeks to heal. Panicked by this inexplicable sight, I threw open my bedroom door and rushed into the bathroom, careless of how much noise I might be causing. Immediately, I turned the sink on and had it pouring the coldest water it could. Frantically, I begin to splash it against my face, occasionally pausing to stare at myself in the mirror. With each splash, I became more and more distressed. 'Why am I not waking up?" I found myself wondering. I grabbed my arm between two of my fingers and pinched down as hard as I could. This method failed likewise. I came to terms with it: I was awake.

Despite the inexplicable nature of what I was experiencing, I found myself not nearly as frightened or panicked now. I took a few deep breaths before stepping out of the bathroom and back into my room. Quickly, I changed into my clothes for the day and headed downstairs. It came as quite a startle to me that when I got downstairs, Pa was nowhere to be found. He almost always was up and finishing up breakfast by the time I got down here. Curious, I went up to the living room window and peered outside, scanning the farm to see if I could spot him, but I didn't. The confusion began to sweep over me as I started to think that perhaps he went into town to get something. But just as I was starting to rationalize his absence in my head, I heard a creaking sound upstairs.

My destination became the staircase as I felt my head tilting up to see what was going on. Just as I was able to see up the steps, I caught a faint glimpse of Pa going into the bathroom. Had he just woken up? Hunger began to take its toll on me as I considered the strong possibility that Pa would not want to spend any time making breakfast. He would not, as he would see it, waste any more time of the morning not out working. I seated myself at the kitchen table in my designated chair as the sound of Pa's boots against the hardwood of the stairs began to grow in volume as he got closer. We exchanged glances as he stepped into the kitchen. Initially, he said nothing. He merely went up to one of the cabinets and grabbed from inside it two slices of bread.

Adding nothing more to them, he began to viscerally shove a bite into his mouth. After what felt like an eternity of silence with me sitting at the table quietly and him chewing away at his food, he finally swallowed before speaking.

"I overslept... so there's no time to cook. Just make yourself something,' he proclaimed, not making eye contact but instead staring out the kitchen window toward the woods. I listened to his request and got up out of my chair, prepared to find something to eat for myself. Pa walked into the living room, finishing up the final bites of his bread slices.

I stepped up to the same cabinet that Pa opened and grabbed, likewise, two slices of bread from a full loaf. However, I was determined to eat something more than just this. As such, I also grabbed a jar of peanut butter and spread some of it onto both slices. As I chewed on the sandwich, Pa stepped outside and immediately started working. I needed to eat quickly for I knew Pa would want me outside as soon as possible to help him. As such, I scarfed down the rest of the sandwich, threw on my boots, and scurried out the front door.

I stepped outside and was greeted with the blinding light, along with the exhausting heat, of the sun. When I was a young child, Pa would always tell me that I would get used to the heat, but I never did. My boots made a thud against the wooden porch as I made my way down the steps and onto the dry dirt of the farm. Off in the distance, I observed Pa stepping inside the barn, presumably in search of the cows to collect milk. For a brief moment, I found myself yet again entranced by the woods in the distance. It was as though being outside and working became more bearable, merely because it allowed me to be closer to them.

I quickly escaped my trance, recalling that Pa had already assigned me my task last night at dinner: I needed to retrieve the tractor which had been left out in the middle of the field. This also reminded me of how painfully tense our conversation was last night and prompted me to conclude that today was not the day to cause any problems with Pa. So, I got to work immediately. I made my pilgrimage across what felt like a mile-long journey toward the center of the field. By the time I reached the tractor, I was already sweating profusely.

I started to examine it, looking for the key to start it. It didn't take long, as the key had been conveniently left dangling in the ignition, waiting, yearning to be turned. I planted myself into the tractor's seat, turned the key, and began to carefully drive it toward the barn. Cars always scared me, the thought of driving them on a busy road filled me with anxiety. But there was a joy in driving the tractor through the field. There were no rules to follow, nobody else around you to worry about, just a free range of motion. This caused me to, in a rare moment, actually enjoy the work I was doing out here.

As I drove, I suddenly realized that Pa was no longer

inside the barn. Instead, he was out on the field near me. He wasn't going toward me, however, or even looking at me. He was standing near one of the field's edges, kicking around the dirt underneath his feet, as though he were looking for something buried. As I watched him search rather aimlessly, I brought the tractor to a stop as I remembered what was near where Pa was standing. Almost involuntary, I felt myself holler at him.

"Careful, there's a scythe around there!" I proclaimed as he looked up at me abruptly with a confused look on his face.

"What?" he yelled back before slowing himself down and carefully examining the ground around him.

I became worried. "What about the blood?" I thought to myself. "Is it still there? What's he gonna think?" I started to examine the area around him as well, though I was handicapped by the distance. I looked to the patch of land between the field and the woods. To my amazement and relief, the trail of blood that I had dragged with me last night was gone. I could only hope that the blood would be gone inside the field as well.

I started driving the tractor toward Pa, desperate to see what he was seeing. As I approached him, he crouched down on the ground to examine something. I brought the tractor to a stop, hopped out, and ran over to him. Once I reached him, I looked over his shoulder. He was not examining blood, as there was none to be found. He was examining the scythe which lay on the ground, just as I had told him. Its blade was also devoid of blood. Pa lifted himself up from his crouched position and looked at me. The slightest of grins formed across his face.

"Maybe you do pay a little attention around here after all," he stated with an almost, but not quite, proud inflection. His grin faded as soon as he finished his statement. He turned around and started walking back toward the barn. I found my eyes darting back and forth between him and the scythe which he left on the ground.

"Guess I'll pick it up myself," I muttered to myself, mildly aggravated. I grabbed the scythe and set it in a tucked away compartment of the tractor before getting back in the seat and driving it fully out of the field. Next to the barn were two other tractors of different colors and sizes from the one I was driving. Next to them was an open spot, waiting to be taken by the one I was driving. I drove it into its designated position and turned it off. The key remained in the ignition as I could not be sure where Pa would want it.

I stepped out of the tractor and picked up the scythe, carrying it with me into the barn. Upon stepping inside, I made my way over to a rack that harbored a series of farm tools. There was a vacant spot that I hooked the scythe onto. I was bewildered to hear and see Pa on the upper floor of the barn. He was cleaning a series of wooden pillars that went up to the roof. Having expected to see Pa milking the cows, I went over to them to see if he had already finished with that. He had, on the contrary, failed to even start that task. There was a series of empty buckets near the cows, none of which had begun to be filled.

"Haven't gotten to it yet," Pa said, cleaning the pillars and avoiding eye contact. "You can do it; I know you know how," he finished. I found myself deeply agitated by Pa's skewed priorities. Regardless of how I felt, I knew that I needed to keep my promise to myself that I would stay on his good side. So, rather than responding, I took a seat next to one of the cows and planted a bucket underneath it.

The rest of the day became something of a blur. It was distinctly exhausting, for I found myself doing what felt like more work than I had ever done before. Pa had declared today the day of mundane tasks, which left me with all the heavy lifting and dirty work. I felt my body go on autopilot about halfway through it, and I couldn't recall if either of us had ever even stopped for a lunch break during all of it.

By the time we were finished, and Pa declared the work complete for the day, the sun was beginning to set and I was drenched in sweat, yearning for a shower. As we made our way back into the house, it set in just how late in the day it was, and how little energy I had left. A wave of defeat washed over me as I questioned whether I would be able to muster the energy for any painting on this night. A voice in my head spoke with great confidence that I would fail to even grab the brush or sit down at my desk.

We got inside and Pa's first destination became the living room sofa. He plopped himself down and, at least for the moment, remained rather content doing nothing but gazing at the bookshelf in front of him. My mind became filled with horrific images of his sweat covered clothes seeping into the fabric beneath him. I couldn't understand how he could possibly be so comfortable keeping himself in that disgusting, dirty state. As for me, my destination was the shower. I readied myself to go upstairs, but just before I could begin my ascent to the cleansing waters, Pa brought me to a stop with his words.

"I need one more thing from you," he said, keeping his head facing forward toward the bookshelf, not even aiming his eyes toward me. I stood still and stared toward him with as attentive of a gaze as I could muster. All I could hope for in that moment was for his task to be a brief, simple one. "Go up to my room. There's a book on my desk I've meant to bring down here." I made sure to keep my emotions hidden from him, but inside a flurry of excitement shot through me at this request. Pa's room was a strictly forbidden place almost all of the time. The only exceptions were moments like this when I was specifically ordered to enter. I got a great deal of pleasure from stretching out these opportunities as much as possible, granting myself the opportunity to explore his room. Using my newfound energy from the excitement, I scurried up the stairs in pursuit of the forgotten book.

I reached the top of the steps and turned to face Pa's room. The door, composed of terribly chipped wood and white paint, was closed. Even with permission to enter, there was a fair part of me that approached the door with reverence. I slowly reached my hand out and turned the round, brass handle. The door creaked open as the room revealed itself. It was exceptionally hard to make out any details, as the only light in the room was coming from the setting sun through the closed blinds of a window. I rubbed my hand against the wall, feeling for the light switch. Within a brief moment, I found it and flicked it on.

The room became vibrantly illuminated by the warm, yellow light in the center of the room. In the back right corner of the room was a bed adorned with gray sheets, pillows, and a blanket of the same color. It was a king size bed whose usage was clearly confined to just half as the blankets on one side were rustled and fixed on the other. The room, in its entirety, was plagued with an overwhelming feeling of emptiness that didn't match the level of furnishing and space it carried. There were two dressers, both adorned with decorations atop them. One of the dressers was an off-white, yellow tinted color. It had a round mirror hanging above it on the wall, complimented with floral decorations around its frame. On this dresser were two pictures.

The first picture was of two people: it was Pa and Mom. They are sitting next to one another on a wooden stump in a vibrant, colorful meadow of sorts. Their hands are locked together, and both of their faces are adorned with the greatest of smiles. I couldn't remember the last time I had seen Pa smile so big... so sincerely. The second picture was of three people: the whole family. There I was, standing in between Mom and Pa. Mom was wearing a wonderful red dress while Pa and I were both wearing a suit. I was still in my youth at the time, not even five feet tall yet. Mom had her arm wrapped around me as all three of us smiled big for the camera. Pa's smile was just as sincere as it was in the other picture. Both of these pictures were placed at angles that seemed to deliberately ensure they did not face the bed directly.

I let out a small sigh. There were no family photos to be found anywhere else in the house. On some level, it was nice to not be given constant reminders about Mom, but it made the rare times I was reminded of her that much more painful. I made my way over to the other dresser. It was composed of a dark brown color. Upon a haphazard analysis, one may even assume it was black. There was no mirror hanging above it, nor were there a slew of decorations across the top of it. There were even fewer pictures on it than the other dresser, as there was only one. It was a picture of two people...Mom and Pa. They stood next to one another, though there was a considerable gap between them. They were both dressed somewhere between casual and formal, as Pa wore a flannel and jeans while Ma wore a button up and suit pants. Their smiles were as large as they were in both of the previous pictures.

I began to feel the horrific, involuntary feeling of water welling up in my eyes as my throat tightened and my breathing became heavy. A flurry of emotions rushed through me. Feelings of anger, sadness, longing, and reminiscing all at once overtaking me, submitting me into an awfully vulnerable position. Quickly, I lifted my hands up toward my eyes and began to rub at them aggressively. I forced myself to cough, followed by clearing my throat, as though I was purging the physical feeling of the lump that the tears carried with them. I closed my eyes and took a few deep breaths, pulling myself together. This time spent paused, returning to the moment, reminded me that I still had a task to complete. I opened my eyes back up and looked over at a corner of the room where Pa's desk sat. It was a desk composed of hollow metal bars and wooden planks and drawers. It was painted gray all around, save for the drawer handles which were a distinct, polished black.

There was little on top of the desk. There was a small lamp and some roughly handled papers that had a barrage of math problems written on them. I could make out a few words among the chicken scratches that were Pa's handwriting: "Corn...Loss...Profit." None of this mattered to me. All I was here for was the book that lay next to the papers. It was a book with a soft, red cover. It did not have a title on it that I could find. The book's fore-edge was sealed with a lock that prevented it from being opened.

As I grabbed the book, I was nearly prepared to commit to leaving the room. I had already spent too much time here, and I knew Pa would soon start investigating what was taking me so long. However, I could not help but come to a stop as my eyes caught a glimpse of one of the desk drawers that was not closed all the way. On the inside of the drawer, I saw glimpses of paper. Paper with splotches of color on it. I reached out my hand, gripped the drawer handle, and slowly pulled it open.

The opened drawer revealed a painting. A painting that I had started, but not completed. I recalled wondering where it had gone at one point. It was wrinkled terribly, seemingly shoved in the drawer and neglected. My hand, shaking, lifted the painting up, prepared to examine the horrific sight up close. But before I could properly examine it, my eyes darted back inside the drawer to see another painting of mine sitting beneath the one in my hand. It was just as damaged and carelessly handled. I lifted up the second painting to see a third one beneath it, and beneath that one, a fourth one. It felt, in my mind, as though the pile would go on forever. I could hardly decide if I wanted to see how deep it went. My decision, however, was quickly made for me as I started to hear Pa's boots coming up the stairs.

With a speed beyond which I thought was possible of me, if any human, I pushed the despair ridden thoughts that the sight of these paintings had imbued in me out of my mind. I frantically pushed the paintings back into the drawer, having little regard for their wellbeing as the damage was already done. I closed the drawer and turned to walk toward the doorway. Just as I was about to get through the threshold, Pa appeared and stopped me right at the edge of the room. Initially, he simply stared me down, saying nothing. After what felt like an eternity of silent, merciless judgment, his eyes began to pan down toward my hand holding the book. His eyes no longer interlocked with mine. I was able to take one small breath before he darted his gaze back into me.

"Take it downstairs," he commanded, his voice cold and calculating. Saying nothing, I began to shift my body around him as the door to his room slammed shut behind me. I didn't want to know what he was thinking, nor did I want to talk to him. All I could hope was that he genuinely believed I struggled to find the book that was sitting so obviously on the desk. I got downstairs to the bookshelf before coming to a stop.

Staring it down, I realized that I was not sure where to put it. I more or less froze up, waiting for Pa to give me further instructions. He arrived back downstairs and, from the corner of his eye, saw me waiting for him to say something. He walked into the kitchen before raising his voice to give his order: "Put it wherever you can find a spot." I obliged him and put the book in the first open spot I could find.

The rest of the evening became something of a blur.

All I could recall was the relieving feeling of water purging me of the sweat and grime of the day's work, followed by a goulash of food-like items serving as dinner. The most distinct feature of the night was what it was missing: creativity. I went up to my room for bed feeling a sense of defeat and, more than that, a sense of guilt at having not done any painting for the day. As much as my mind would allow it, I tried to forgive myself, attempting to reassure my mind that it was a physically and emotionally exhausting day, a day that had shown me how Pa truly felt about my paintings. As I crawled into bed, there was a repetitive, intrusive thought that entered my mind, proclaiming that I shouldn't paint any more. I blocked it out every time it emerged, but it would always find its way back. The stress this caused me forced my feet back onto the ground of my room as I started pacing, as though I wanted to wear myself out even further to stop my mind from thinking anything at all. During my futile efforts to silence my mind, my eyes went out the window toward my source of solace: the trees.

What was I to do now? The cold sight of the tree silhouettes against the dark sky somehow still managed to harbor a warm feeling, an irresistible feeling. It felt as though I would never get to sleep now, for I wanted nothing more than to return to them. I considered that Pa had gone to bed before I did. It was possible he was still not quite asleep yet. However, in my mind, the risk was one I was willing, no…one I had to take. I threw on some proper clothes and, before opening my bedroom door, said a mediocre prayer that the sound of Pa's TV would drown out my footsteps if he were still awake. I made my way into the hall and crept down the steps, physically hurting from every creak that sounded off from the wood. I made it to the front door, anxiously opened it, and off I went toward my sanctuary.

I had not gone to sleep this time. There was no convincing myself that this was a dream, or that I was sleepwalking or hallucinating. This was real, and I was doing this by choice. As I got closer to the sea of trees, I started to see visions in my mind of the beast. Though my only experience with the beast was it attacking me, I felt a yearning to have another interaction with it. When I first saw it, I was so certain that it had to be nothing more than my overactive imagination, but I knew that, if I saw it again, I would not be so sure.

I longed to know more about the beast. Had it always been here? If so, why was I just now seeing it? What was its purpose? It was a monolith of mystique and a beacon of confusion. As I came within no more than twenty feet of the tree line, the distinct, powerful sound of steps against the ground began to emit from within the entanglement of branches. It was only moments later that the beast emerged once again. It stared at me with its stern blue eyes as it remained stationary. I took pride and comfort in the fact that I was far less intimidated by it this time. Rather than coming closer to me, the beast turned itself around and slowly started walking back into the trees. On some level, my sense of control over my own body appeared to dissipate in this moment, as I felt my legs closing the gap between myself and the beast.

As I entered the complex of wood that was the forest, I allowed the gleaming, galactic glow of the beast's ax and attire to guide me. I looked on in awe at the beauty of the environment around me. Now that I was inside the trees, it was inexplicably bright and easy to see everything around me. It was not as though it was day, nor was it as though it was night. The sky was a cool, turquoise shade that made the woods visible and calming, but certainly not natural. My legs continued to be an independent agent from the rest of my body, carrying me along so as to keep up with the beast. It walked with a slow, calm, and confident gate. It felt no need to look behind it to see if I had followed; either because it was so certain I was following, or because it did not care whether I was or not.

It wasn't until we reached what felt like the heart of the forest, the absolute center point where getting out would take a millennium, that we finally came to a stop. Though this location, due to its incredibly isolated feeling, carried an eerie presence, it was still awe-inspiringly beautiful. There was the distinct sound of water flowing due to a small, steady stream that flowed between two rows of rocks and went underground. There was a series of bushes, all adorned with flowers of various shapes and colors. The trees were towering constructs whose every flaw, from heavy moss to broken branches, felt deliberate and enhancing in beauty. Complimenting so much beauty in the environment were various beautiful species whom it was a privilege to be around.

Wandering through the landscape a mere fifteen feet away was a deer who lacked antlers. It was absolutely and entirely aware of my presence, but it was not bothered by me. A flock of doves traversed and pecked around at the ground, equally calm around me. A black horse with a gray marking along its head seemingly manifested as it started to contently drink from the water of the river. Atop a tree branch some twenty feet in the air was the ultimate sight. A bird's nest which housed a group of red baby birds who periodically chirped to one another.

As I walked around, staring with reverence at all that was around me, I thought about how I had never been so happy to be outside. I had come to associate the outdoors with nothing but labor, and the inside of the house with where I was truly happy. But now, as I gazed at everything around me, it felt as though I had entered that which made me happy, that I had entered a painting.

Located near the stream of water was a large tree stump. I walked over to it and planted myself onto it. The beast stared off into the distance, paying no attention neither to me nor to the beauty of everything around it. I found myself entranced by the beast, committing all of my focus to staring at it and taking in every detail. It seemed not to care about being watched at all. After a few moments, it started to walk around the general area, with no destination or goal in mind. I kept watching the beast move about. An endless barrage of questions went through my mind about the beast. But what was I to do? The idea of simply asking the beast any one of the questions felt like a fool's errand. But as time passed and both of us sat in silence, I became less content to just take in the area around me, and I desired more; I desired to communicate directly with the beast. I took a deep breath, readying myself for the defiant, dangerous act of speaking to it, wishing to avoid sounding nervous in my inflection.

"So, what are you?" I asked in as firm of a tone as I

could muster. The creature came to a screeching halt with its back to me. I involuntarily felt myself swallow heavily. Images went through my mind of the beast lifting its ax and sending it over my head again. But this is not what happened.

The beast slowly turned around to look at me. It took a few steps toward me but stopped once there was about six feet between us. It turned its ax and planted it straight into the ground with the handle pointing toward the sky. It gripped both of its hands on the handle as it stared down at the ground that stood between us.

"What you are asking, most importantly, is whether I am real or not," the beast proclaimed with its ethereal voice that seemed to be heard from all directions. I was too frightened to respond, but internally I took this to be a fair analysis of what I was looking for. "I am something in between your broad sense of reality and fantasy. I am something not of this world nor this plane of reality." This response provided me with something to cling to, something which gave me enough confidence to attempt to put some pieces together for myself.

"So, you're some kind of alien?" I asked, almost feeling my eyes light up, waiting for reinforcement from the beast. Its initial response was to look up at me.

"I am not referring to the physical world you exist in. I am referring to your individual world that you experience... the world that no one else experiences nor understands," it started, turning its gaze to look off into the distance. "I am real, and I can affect you." It turned back to stare directly into my eyes. "But only in *your* world." This explanation was cryptic, but it did help me start to understand the nature of this beast. I was utterly compelled to ask more questions now.

"Why am I just now seeing you? Have you always existed in my world?" With a speed that trumps light, the beast darted right up to my face. Though it did not touch me, it startled me to the point that I fell backwards off of the stump. I lay in the grass, staring up at the beast with fear in my eyes.

"Do not be so arrogant!" it started. "I am here because you need me... and only while you need me." The beast let out a small huff of air from its nostrils before turning around and slowly walking away from the stump. I slowly began to bring myself back onto my feet, trying to conceal an expression of anger and contempt that I now felt toward the beast. I had to understand that this was no human being I was in a dialectical war with. This was not someone who could be reasoned with nor someone who would have any concern for their behavior upsetting me. I pulled myself together emotionally and prepared to speak again. I was determined to cautiously challenge the beast's claim.

"How exactly do I need you?" I inquired. The beast opted out of any kind of oral response. He simply kept walking and pulled his ax out of the ground. From the tree branch above us, the baby birds in the nest began to fly away. I waited anxiously for the beast to say something, anything, but it wouldn't. In my determination to keep a conversation afloat and obtain as much information about the beast as I could, I made the hazardous decision to make a playful, if not passive aggressive comment. "Don't minotaurs usually live in some kind of maze?" I deliberated what the word was I was looking for. "What is it called, a labyrinth?" I proclaimed. The beast responded with a spiteful sound, almost as though it were smirking, though I could not see its face. It turned around once again to face me.

"What are these woods if not a maze... a labyrinth of their own?" the beast asked rhetorically. "You are in a maze with an infinite number of ways to escape. All you must do is keep moving, and you will eventually find yourself outside of it." I found it conflicting as to whether I should embrace the cryptic, ambiguous nature of the beast's response, or if I should allow myself to smirk and reveal how ridiculous I found it.

It was at this point that we both went silent for a while. I certainly was not ready for my time with the beast to end, but I wanted time to reflect on what had been said so far. The part of our conversation, if I'm to generously call it that rather than a confrontation, that lingered in my mind most came from one of the earliest comments made by the beast. When it discussed how it existed in only *my* world. As I reflected on this comment, I started to feel more comfortable around the beast, and a thirst grew inside of me that could only be quenched by opening my heart up to it. I did not desire to open up to the beast because I trusted it, as I did not. I felt the desire because I was certain that the beast could do nothing with what I would tell it other than respond. There was no one for it to spread rumors to, no way for it to use the information to hurt me later in life. All it had was me, right now, in the present moment. How to approach the beast about this was an enigma. It had proven itself capable and, indeed, excellent at communicating, but it was unlikely to be congruent with what I was looking for, that is, empathetic and caring. All I could do was try, and hope that the beast would surprise me.

"How much do you know about me? My life, my interests, my thoughts. What all are you aware of?" I asked, for the first time speaking with genuine confidence. The beast did not hesitate to respond.

"Everything. I know everything that could possibly be known about you. Every moment of every day since you were born. Every thought that has crossed your mind. Every desire that you have had and every source of joy and pain that you have come across in your life." This answer was both frightening and comforting. The beast knowing everything about me felt invasive, but it gave me newfound confidence that I could talk about anything, and it would, perhaps, know something about me that not even I myself knew.

"So can you talk to me about my father?" I felt myself ask. The words came out of me with the same awful, involuntary feeling as a vile purge. Much like a purge, however, it needed to come out. The beast snarled; I could even see a faint grin come across its face from the side view I had of it.

"What do you want me to do?" it asked with a tone that antagonized my question.

"I'm not looking for you to *do* anything, I just want you to listen," I revolted, annoyed by its confrontational tone. The beast turned itself toward me. I felt myself quake with fear, trembling in anticipation for the beast to charge at me once again. Instead, it walked up to me slowly. Most shockingly, once it had reached me, it got down onto one knee so as to be eye level with me.

"Your pride is blinding you," it started, adopting the most nurturing cadence that I had seen from it. "You desperately want someone to help you. You don't just want me to listen. You want me to say something that will bring about an enlightenment for you." I felt a flurry of emotions starting to brew within me. "You are begging for magical words that will change your perspective and heal your broken relationship with your father." My face began to grow hot with anger.

"Stop it, stop it," I begin to mutter to myself.

"You are begging to have the kind of family you used to have... nurturing, warm, and accepting."

"Stop it, stop it." My volume grew louder.

"There is nothing I can say to give you what you want."

"Stop it. Stop it."

"There is nothing you can do to have what you want."

"Stop it. Stop it."

"What you want is gone, forever. You will never have what you once had ever again."

"STOP IT!" I hollered with a voice of unyielding pain and defensive anger. I fell down onto my knees as tears poured from my eyes. The beast brought itself back onto both feet. It sat in silence, looking down at me as I lay in shambles.

"Understand something," the beast started, taking a few steps away from me. "Your father is not a monster. Whether you recognize it or understand it or not, he has always loved you." I was far too broken to respond to this assertion. But I knew, in my heart of hearts, that the beast was wrong. It could proclaim its ultimate wisdom about me as much as it wished. It could be correct in all its other beliefs and observations about my life. But on this, it was wrong.

I lay on the ground with my hands covering my face. I felt the beast's hooves step up to me. I gathered as much strength as I could to pull my hands away and look up at the beast who I was sure was looking down at me with contempt. I slowly moved my hands to see the beast gazing at me, but not with contempt. It was stoic… entirely devoid of any judgment of my behavior. I felt strangely comforted by this. However, just as this comfort was beginning to harbor in me, the beast lifted its ax. My eyes filled with fear just before it sent the ax down onto my head.

3

I awoke in a frenzy much too similar to the previous day's rude awakening. By some divine intervention I had managed to not topple out of my bed onto the floor.

Within a few moments, after I recovered from my initial shock, I came to a state of peculiar calm, understanding this time what had just happened. I knew for utterly certain that I had not woken up from a dream, for I had never gone to sleep. Still, though, I found myself wondering with baited-breath why the beast felt the need to make its means of sending me back to my home so traumatic. Perhaps it had no other option. I readied myself to get out of bed. However, before I could properly begin the process I was disrupted by a sudden sound from the ceiling above me.

My eyes peered up toward the ceiling to witness my painting coming loose from the tape which had been used to keep it stationed. On some level, I knew that this was not a catastrophe by any means. I knew, deep down, that the painting could be taped right back up. And yet, despite this, I felt my face take on an involuntary expression of horror as I looked up, seemingly frozen with fear at the sight of it preparing to fall. As the paper finally broke free entirely, time slowed down as the paper gently swayed through the air, down onto my bed.

I slowly lifted the painting off of the blanket which I saw as its grave. As I analyzed the painting, I felt a new level of connection to the visual of the birds flying out of the nest, now that it was not merely an image which I had conjured in my head but something which I had witnessed in the real world with my own eyes, if I was to call the world that the beast showed me the *real* world. I threw my blankets off of me and rose up from the bed. With the painting in my hand, I readied to leave the room and headed for my door.

When I emerged through the doorway, I was immediately hit with an utterly foreign, foul odor which I could not describe. My face shriveled up with contempt for the onslaught of horror that was assaulting my nostrils. Using my free hand that wasn't holding the painting, I covered my mouth and pinched my nose as I started to make my way down the stairs. My hand, however, failed to offer any kind of reprieve. With each step that I took down the staircase, the stench grew in intensity, overpowering all of my feeble attempts to stop it. As soon as I reached the bottom of the steps I spotted Pa in the kitchen and hurried over to him.

"What on earth is that awful stench?" I asked him. He did not turn to look at me, he was preoccupied with writing something down on a small piece of paper. His face, however, gave off the exceptional impression that he was not nearly as affected by the smell as I was.

"The window," he muttered. My face became a mixture of confusion and disgust as I started to look around at all of the windows. Once my eyes reached the living room, I spotted what he most certainly had to be referring to: one of them was open. "For some reason you had the brilliant idea of leaving it open last night... Plenty of time for the stench of the barn to seep in here," he explained. Without hesitation, I rushed over to the window and slammed it shut. The smell still lingered, but I had to hope it would dissipate soon enough. As I started to make my way back to the kitchen, I felt myself become thoroughly confused by the accusation that I had left the window open. I could not recall at any point opening it in the first place. Had I done it before I left to confront the beast? It certainly didn't sound familiar. Had the beast itself somehow opened the window? Perhaps, I thought, but what motivation would it have to do something so peculiar?

Before I reached the kitchen, I stopped at my painting table next to the other living room window. I placed the painting of the birds onto it, declaring that I would tape it back up after breakfast. I made my way into the kitchen and grabbed my seat at the table. Pa continued to write on the piece of paper before beginning to speak.

"Today is a rest day," he proclaimed. "You can focus on..." He let out a sigh in the midst of his sentence. "Whatever that is you like wasting your time on." The crude comment thoroughly annoyed me, but I managed to ignore such furious thoughts and instead focused on the joy I had of knowing I didn't have to do any farm work today. Pa finished writing on the piece of paper, folded it up, and put it in his pocket. He then walked over to the table and planted himself into his chair. I couldn't help but look confused by this. He had not made any food, not even for himself. Even more strangely he didn't have anything to drink.

"Are you not hungry?" I asked.

"God damn it boy!" he hollered, crashing his fist onto the table, sending a tremor of fear through me. "I just told you that you don't have to do any work today and the first thing you do is go on and ask me to make breakfast for you," he explained with a return to his regular, calm, and cold tone. I was terribly frightened, but utterly compelled to try to stand up for myself.

"That's not what I was saying. I just wondered why you didn't—" My sentence was cut short.

"Make something yourself," he asserted. I went silent, bringing my eyes down toward the table. My eyes started to well up as I harnessed everything in me to resist the insatiable desire to cry. I rubbed my eyes with my hand, trying to make it appear more so like I was annoyed rather than upset. In the midst of this, however, I begin to feel myself genuinely switching from a feeling of hurt to a feeling of anger. My head slowly lifted up to stare Pa down with an expression of fury and contempt...of hatred.

"Why do you treat me this way?" a voice asked, a voice that no doubt emitted from me, and yet one so bold that I failed to recognize it as sincerely coming from my own soul. As I sat there, however, staring my father down with such contempt, I began to feel myself returning to the moment. I began to feel myself embracing what I had just said and reveling in it. Pa's face immediately grew red with anger, but he did not yell in his response.

"You think I've treated you badly? You don't have the first clue about what that would be like." My face took on an expression of deeper, vengeful anger.

"Maybe... But I know what it's like to be treated well." I paused, taking a metaphorical deep breath internally. "Mom treated me well, unlike you."

"Is that right? What did she do that was so different?" I found myself furious at such a feigning of ignorance. How could he be so deliberately obtuse and not recognize the obvious differences?

"Maybe that she made me feel like I actually meant something? Or that she would actually show me some goddamn affection from time to time?" I paused briefly, assessing what else I wanted, no, needed to say. "At least she was invested in me. My interests were her interests and she cheered me on for my accomplishments. Whereas you... you just look down on me constantly. I can't think of one time where you showed support for my interests... And I guess that's why you hide my paintings in your room."

"Enough!" Pa roared, rising up quickly from his chair. "You know nothing of what you're talking about. You're more ignorant than you can possibly imagine. Stop now before you make an even bigger fool out of yourself." I felt an utterly involuntary laugh emit from me.

"And off you go, immediately proving my point further," I started. "You refuse to listen to anything I have to say. You won't hear me out or even consider the possibility that you might, somehow, be in the wrong about something."

"Keep lying to me and yourself all you want, you fool," he proclaimed, lowering his voice. "The truth of this matter isn't going anywhere. No matter what you believe, reality will remain here, waiting for you, even if you deny it." A wave of defeat came over me. It became clear in this moment that no matter what I said, no matter how much I said, nothing would get through to Pa. I was speaking to an immovable, brick wall with anger that flowed through its veins of cement.

"Fine. Maybe someday you'll realize that you're the one denying reality," I muttered with a calm tone, realizing that my ferocious anger had gotten me nowhere.

Pa said nothing. He just stood, waiting for me to make my next move. And so I did. With my head down to the floor, I walked around him and out of the kitchen. I made my way upstairs, my soul cracking further and further with each creak of the wood beneath me. I arrived at my room and closed the door before heading to my bed and lying in it.

As I lay there, creating for myself what felt like a watery grave as tears streamed down my face and onto my blanket on either side of me, I rolled flat onto my back so as to stare up at the ceiling. The ceiling was nothing but a blur within the watery lens I was plagued with. I lifted my hands up and wiped away the tears. They would inevitably return, but it provided me with a brief window to see clearly. And there, against all odds, I became even more distressed than I already was. The horrific sight of the blank ceiling above my bed sent chills over me. My symbol of solace, my visual of comfort, my painting, it was gone. Now it lay downstairs, out of literal and metaphorical reach.

It was my expectation that this would only strengthen the flow of my tears. But, with great uncertainty as to whether it was a blessing or a curse, this is not what happened. The longer I stared at the blank ceiling, the more my tears faded away, replaced with a heavy panting of a soul on the edge. A soul filled with smoldering rage that could not be extinguished. All at once, my mind escaped from its state Pa had placed me in, a state of giving up. I was more motivated than ever. I knew exactly what I had to do, and I had to do it now; there was no time, in my mind, to wait for nightfall.

Like a child arising from a nightmare, I aggressively shot up out of my bed. My mind would not allow me to do anything, or even consider doing anything, other than what was now my ultimate objective. Methodically, I cracked open my bedroom door. My eyes glanced around like prey in search of a camouflaged predator. A sense of relief came over me as I observed the empty hallway and a clear path to my destination: Pa's bedroom door. This euphoric state was enhanced when I heard the sounds of footsteps downstairs, somewhere in the kitchen. I knew now that my plan, as risky as it was, could be executed if I remained cautious. Slowly, I extended my foot out onto the wooden floor. As I shifted my weight on top of it, the faintest of creaks emitted from the surface beneath me, causing me to close my eyes and tense up. This brief period of silence left me waiting anxiously to hear Pa make his way toward the stairs, but he didn't.

I was captivated by a mixture of two directly opposed emotions. I was filled with fear at what might happen with my next steps and hope for what these steps would mean for me. Ultimately, hope won out as my feet started moving forward again. Some steps were silent, others emitted a light creak of their own. But with each noise that failed to get Pa's attention, my confidence grew. After the odyssey that was the ten feet between my room and Pa's, I arrived at his doorway. I slowly turned the handle of the door and was blessed by its graceful silence as it opened. The journey was not yet over, but the rug that padded the floor of his room made me far less afraid. I made my way along the rug as virtually no noise happened now, and quickly arrived at my true destination: his dresser. My eyes locked onto the picture which had so deeply hurt me the previous day. The picture of him and Mom, with me nowhere in sight.

I reached out and took hold of the picture, clutching it against my chest before turning around to leave the room. With each motion closer to the doorway, images shot through my mind of Pa stopping me just as he had yesterday. But as I reached the doorway, I was ecstatic to find that he remained nowhere in sight. Somehow, the walk back to my room from his felt so much easier; I could swear the floor had become sturdier. Once I was in my room, I quietly closed the door and released the biggest sigh of relief I ever had. There was, however, no time for me to celebrate. There was much to be done, and no time to waste in doing it.

My legs made their way toward my window before my arms placed the picture down onto my bed. I gripped the window with both hands and began to lift it open. Dust flew off the rim with each motion, as though I was opening an ancient tomb buried beneath the earth. It was notably, almost laughably difficult to open, but I succeeded nonetheless. Once the window was out of the way as much as it could be, I picked the picture up off the bed and readied for a journey I never anticipated to take.

Controlling my breathing so as to not panic, I lifted my foot up and out the window. I shifted it around until it found a resting spot on a protruded piece of foundation. My other foot, similarly, managed to be planted on a bump on the side of the house. Carefully, I pulled the rest of my body out of the window, gripping the outside edge of the window with my free hand, and gripping the picture even more tightly in the other hand. I was a mere fifteen feet off the ground, only needing to descend about halfway before I could safely drop down. The presence of the sun allowed me to easily scan the house beneath me to find new spots to shift to. However, the sun also contributed heavily to the physically taxing nature of this feat. With each movement of my body, sweat built up on my forehead like a damp cloth was lying against it. The veins in my free arm were glistening as they had to carry the entire upper half of my body. I worried not about how sweaty I was, or whether I would pop my shoulder out of place moving around in the haphazard way I was. All I cared about was reaching the ground.

After a mere minute or two, which felt ten times that, I stood about five feet off the ground. I gently allowed my feet to slide off their current positions as my body dangled in the air. I looked down at the ground, it was a clear, dry dirt patch. There was no risk any more. I released my hand and went down to the ground. As I fell, I gripped the picture with both hands. My feet made a thud, and I examined the picture to make sure it was still in the same state as when I started the descent. It was. I looked up at the escape hatch that was the open window in my room, before turning toward the woods and jumping into a sprint toward them.

As I ran, I could only imagine what was going to happen when I reached the trees. Would the beast even appear? Would it wonder why I was there during the daytime? Would it welcome me? Once I was a distance out from the front of the house, I briefly turned around to examine it. More than anything, I was checking to make sure Pa was not, by some terribly unfortunate circumstances, outside looking for me. He wasn't. I turned back toward the woods before looking down at the picture as I kept moving.

The fury that it caused me gave me the motivation to move faster and faster with each passing moment. More questions passed through my mind about the beast's inquiries. What would it say to the picture? Would it admit that it was wrong to claim Pa loves me? Will it dismiss the evidence entirely?

As I closed the gap between myself and the woods, clouds began to move in front of the sun. They were not dark, haunting clouds that warned of incoming rain or storm. They were calm clouds that made the journey just a fraction easier. Though I felt great enthusiasm and excitement to see the beast and show it the picture, I could not smile. Far too much anger and resentment flowed through me to muster up a physical display of joy. Nonetheless, the excitement was doing its job by allowing me to complete the trek. And complete it I did, as I reached the trees.

I took my first steps through the beautiful array of nature that had come to be a sanctuary for me. My eyes darted around frantically in search of any indication of the beast, but there was none to be seen. I saw insects scattered about, the occasional small creature running away from me into a hiding spot, and all of it was complemented by the soothing sounds of birds high in the trees who couldn't be spotted. I couldn't properly appreciate any of this, however, as my patience was wearing thin. I was interested in nothing the trees had to offer except for the beast itself.

"I'm here!" I bellowed. My hunch was that the beast may be a great distance away, perhaps even asleep, not expecting my arrival. The sound of my holler echoed through the trees. "Where are you?" I felt the first signs of anxiety and sadness entering me. My throat began to tighten as worrisome thoughts shot through my mind that the beast wouldn't show up. "I have something to show you!" My voice became that of a barter, as though the beast was waiting to be convinced, I was worth its time. There were still no visual or auditory signs of the beast. I looked down at the picture in my hands as I became more desperate. "I need you!" I yelled as loud as my voice would allow me. Even then, however, I was given no reprieve. My body dropped onto its knees in defeat. However, just as I began to give up, my cries were answered.

"Why do you need me?" The beast's all too familiar voice spoke as its message rang down from the sky itself. I rose up to my feet at the new sign of hope.

"You're the only one that can help me," I pleaded, speaking to the sky for I felt that was where the beast was harbored. However, this assumption was quickly broken as the beast's hooves sounded off behind me. It slowly and calmly stepped around me and went a few feet ahead of where I stood before turning to face me.

"It is not *I* who can help you. All I do is provide the truth. So, tell me, will the truth help you?" I sat in silence for a moment. I wasn't sure whether to genuinely consider the question or to be dumbfounded by its strange phrasing.

"Whatever it is that you can give me, that's what I need. If that's the truth then yes, the truth will help me." The beast released a calm huff of air from its nostrils.

"Very well," it affirmed. The beast placed its ax down into the dirt before stepping up close to me. "Why are you here again so soon? The day is still young."

"I couldn't wait. I had to come see you because Pa—"

"Ahh," the beast started, almost with a tone as if it was pleased with itself. "Once again your issue is your father."

"You're wrong about him!" I affirmed. "You said he loves me, but he doesn't! The way he treats me isn't the way a loving father would ever treat his son!"

"You still don't understand. Your father has *always* loved you. It's not what you think." The beast's tone took on a hint of worry.

"It's not what I think? What kind of loving father would neglect me constantly? What kind of loving father would see me as nothing more than the farm work I provide him? What kind of loving father wouldn't even own a picture of me?" I held out the frame with my hands, the picture facing down at the ground. The beast examined it curiously before gently reaching out its hand and taking it. Before lifting the picture up, the beast looked into my eyes.

"Are you sure you want me to see this?" With only brief hesitation, I nodded my head with assurance. The beast lifted its hand up and began to examine the photo. It felt as though time stopped as the beast methodically pondered it. Sweat pooled up in my hands as I anxiously waited for the beast to say something.

"Before I go further. You must look again and see the truth. See...see what you have blocked from your mind." The beast handed the frame back to me with the picture facing up. My soul exorcized itself from my body as I took the picture in my hands. It was as I had seen it before: Mom and Pa were standing on both sides of the picture, smiling, with a gap between them, but the gap was no longer empty. Now I could see it: I was there. I had always been there. I stood between them, smiling all the same. I looked up at the beast and began to step backwards away from it.

"Fear it... hate it... wish it away... That is the truth which you have refused to see. But it was always there."

I couldn't speak. I couldn't look at the beast any longer. I turned around and began to run as fast as I could out of the woods.

"The illusion you've lived in has been easier than reality," the beast spoke, its inescapable voice ringing down from the sky. "You have created a monster you can hate." I began to feel tears coming down my face now. "You hate so you can deny that you have lost what you love." Visions began to shoot through my mind, as the illusion that the beast spoke of began to fall apart within me.

I saw myself sitting with Pa at the kitchen table. He

faded away, out of the seat, as I saw myself carrying conversations and arguing with an empty chair next to me.

I saw myself looking up at Pa with agitation as he did no farm work and left me to do everything, as he slowly faded away, and I saw that I was the only person who had been there to do the work.

I saw the lackluster meals and lack of food that I had blamed Pa for, as it became clear that this wasn't Pa's fault, for he wasn't there to ensure these problems didn't happen.

I saw every moment where I yearned for affection and never received it. It was not because Pa didn't love me, but because he wasn't there.

I saw the paintings which had been placed in the drawer of his desk. Then, I saw images of myself throwing my own paintings into the trash, disappointed in myself. I saw the repressed memory of waking up in the middle of the night to see Pa digging the paintings back out from the bin before taking them to his room. The paintings were not torn up and hidden because Pa hated them. He was proud of my work when I wasn't.

The reality of who Pa was came back to me. Even after Mom had passed, he had done everything for me. I saw every wonderful meal he made for me. I saw every moment of warm, genuine affection he gave me. I saw how much pride he took in my painting, telling me how wonderful my work was. The painting which he had called my best work had ended up on my bedroom ceiling. I saw every warm smile he gave me that I had never known the value of until now. Everything which I felt Pa was keeping from me was a lie. He had kept nothing from me. It wasn't his fault... it wasn't his fault that he had been taken from me.

I burst through the front door of the house. My eyes peered into the living room to see it. Sitting on the couch was Pa's body. His soul had left his body days ago. I ran to the couch and knelt down next to him, holding his cold body against me as tears ran down my face uncontrollably. A gust of wind came through the open door and blew my painting off the desk and onto the floor below me. I continued to sob and hold onto Pa for as long as I could, as tears dripped off my face and onto the birds preparing to leave their nest.